NIMONA

NIMONA

NOELLE STEVENSON

HARPER TEEN

An Imprint of HarperCollinsPublishers

HarperTeen is an imprint of HarperCollins Publishers.

Nimona
Copyright © 2015 by Noelle Stevenson
All rights reserved. Printed in Canada.
No part of this book may be used or reproduced in any manner whatsoever
without written permission except in the case of brief quotations embodied in
critical articles and reviews. For information address HarperCollins
Children's Books, a division of HarperCollins Publishers,
195 Broadway, New York, NY 10007.
www.epicreads.com

The artist used Adobe Photoshop to create the digital illustrations for this book.
Typography by Erin Fitzsimmons
21 22 23 24 TC 20 19 18 17
❖
First Edition

To all the monster girls

CHAPTER 1

1

CHAPTER 2

4

We were friends once. Heroes in training.

We were the two most promising heroes the Institution had ever seen.

until the day of the joust.

We'd never been pitted against each other before.

I knocked him clean off his horse.

It was a fair victory.

but Ambrosius hates to lose.

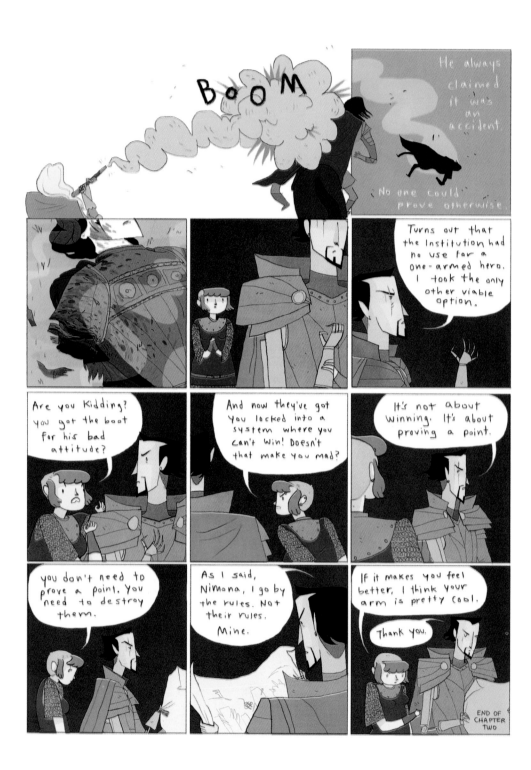

CHAPTER 3

WOOP   WOOP   WOOP   WOOP   WOOP

Squires are always more trouble than they're worth, aren't they?

Dammit, Nimona...

Hold up there, Villain! We've got to fight because that's my job!

Get out of my way.

HAVE AT THEE!

CLANG

You should go. There will be more guards here any minute.

LIVE

EXPLOSION AT LABORATORY

...is believed to be the work of renowned supervillain Ballister Blackheart. The number of casualties has not yet been confirmed...

INCOMING CALL

((( )))

DIRECTOR

Institution of Law Enforcement & Heroics

Some heist you pulled today, Blackheart.

What do you want?

The body count seems... uncharacteristic of you.

It didn't go according to plan.

You don't say.

Have they found any survivors yet?

Your sidekick? She didn't make it out. We made sure of that.

Then it was your people who set off the self-destruct!

We reacted to a potential threat.

She was just a kid!

That's none of our concern.

What kind of person blows up a building to kill one kid? You're a monster.

I'm not a monster.

I'M A SHARK!

AAAAHHH

HA HA HA HA HA

N-Nimona?

HA HA HA HA HA HA HA

DAMN YOU, NIMONA!

Hey, Boss! How ya doing?

You let me think you were dead!

You liiiike me, you were worriiied

You little...

Where are you?

At the Institution headquarters! They don't know I'm here.

Get back here, NOW.

Yeah, okay.

Can I bring all these TOP SECRET plans I found?

Yes! Yes! Just get out of there before they catch you!

You got it, Boss.

And don't EVER do that again.

Hey! You're not authorized to be in here!

Oops, gotta go!

NO NIMONA will you stop doing that!

AAHH

END OF CHAPTER THREE

CHAPTER 4

You can't sleep here, bub. Get a move on.

OUR HERO

20

You completely disregarded my orders!

You went against the plan and made a mess of things!

You almost got yourself killed!

You almost got ME killed!

No offense, but your plan was just gonna end with us getting arrested. I like mine more.

People died in that explosion! Did you even think about that?

We're villains! Villains kill people sometimes!

Killing solves nothing, Nimona.

It's vulgar, it's messy—

If you're going to kill someone, you'd better be sure. You'd better be prepared to accept responsibility.

So I don't KILL people just because they're in my way.

22

Fair enough. We need to cooperate. We need to work as a team.

I will admit that that was some pretty quick thinking in there on your part.

So do I get to help you lay out the next evil plan?

Yes, if you promise to show a little more restraint.

Deal!

POUNCE

You're really good at that.

Thanks!

where did you learn to do that?

How does it work?

I've heard of animal shapeshifters and face-changers, but nothing like this.

What's your story, anyway?

aw man, do I HAVE to do the backstory thing? It's kind of a downer.

'Course, I bet you love downer stories, don't you?

Just tell me.

Fine.

It all started when I was six years old...

I lived with my parents in a tiny village. You know, super normal and boring stuff.

But we were always getting attacked by the raiders from the west.

They'd come without warning, pillaging and burning everything.

I wanted to fight them, but I was only six, and there wasn't a lot I could do.

Then one day I was gathering berries in the woods when I came across a hole in the ground.

HELP

Hey! You okay down there?

25

Alas, I am a poor old woman who has fallen down into this hole.

I am also a witch.

If you help me out, I will give you a magical gift.

If I get you out, can you make me strong enough to defeat the raiders from the west?

Hmmm

I know! I will turn you into a dragon. Then you can fly down and carry me out.

Really? Turn the six-year-old into a dragon? That was her idea?

Just listen to the story, okay?

26

Anyway, it sounded like a good idea at the time.

So she cast the spell and everything went according to plan...

...I became a fearsome dragon.

I carried the witch to safety...

...and saw her on her way.

I was excited to show the village my new dragon's shape, and how strong I had become!

But when I got there, they weren't exactly glad to see me.

The witch had forgotten to show me how to change back, or even how to speak.

I had to run away and find a cave in the woods to hide in.

I spent the next few weeks attempting to change back.

I don't get it. The witch turned you into a dragon—why were you able to become other animals?

The spell was slippery. She wasn't a very good witch.

Well, I'd guessed that much from her brilliant plan of "get out of the hole by turning the six-year-old into a dragon."

Will you please shut up about that?

Finally, I was able to transform back into myself.

I ran home as fast as I could to show my parents what I could do.

But when I got back, I found that the raiders had already come. Everyone from my village was dead, including my parents.

You're right, that _is_ a downer.

Right?

CLUNK

Yessssss

Well, I'm glad we're past the "sob stories" part of our relationship.

Can we order a pizza?

They charge too much to deliver out here.

C'mooon, there's NOTHING edible in your fridge.

There are some genetically altered anchovies in the—

NO.

INSTITUTION OF LAW ENFORCEMENT AND HEROICS

Yes, come in, Sir Goldenloin.

I've been expecting you.

Artist's rendering

I was hoping you could explain all this to me.

It wasn't MY fault. Ballister's new sidekick broke the rules.

Dead

I didn't think she'd be such a problem. She's only a child, after all.

Tell me, how did a child bring about the destruction of our finest research facility right under your very nose?

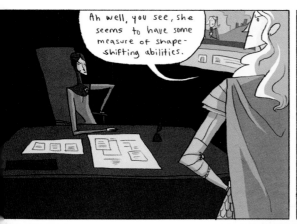

Ah well, you see, she seems to have some measure of shape-shifting abilities.

a SHAPESHIFTER?!

Do you mean to tell me that Ballister Blackheart has a shapeshifter in his employment and you didn't think to mention it until now?

It's only a little one.

It doesn't matter how "little" it is.

This gives him an advantage he didn't have before.

He'll figure that out soon enough.

We cannot allow this.

END OF
CHAPTER FOUR

CHAPTER 5

But how does your shapeshifting WORK? It doesn't make any sense.

It's magic! Can't you just accept it and move on?

No.

Ha, of course not.

"I'm Ballister Blackheart and I only believe in SCIENCE!"

AUGH

Don't do that! It's weird!

Don't do that! It's weird!

Nimona, I swear, if you don't turn back RIGHT NOW—

SSSSSSSCIEEEEENCE

Ha ha! You're so easy to mess with.

I can fire you anytime I want, you know.

Sure, Boss.

Drat this door.

What's wrong with it?

Nothing, it's just very high security.

I've got to enter a series of very precise entry codes, which in turn activate the retinal scanners.

Once the retinal scan is verified, the voice-activation software goes online, and—

KRRASH

37

CLANK

Nimona?
Are you okay?

I'm not going to
run any tests.

Did...did
someone else..?

Ooh!
What's that?

Does it
KILL PEOPLE?

CAN I TRY IT?

DON'T
TOUCH THAT

38

TIME TO SNOOP THROUGH THE INSTITUTION'S STUFF!

Let's see what they consider "top secret plans," shall we?

Aw, these aren't secret plans! It's just a bunch of gibberish!

What a rip-off!

It's encoded.

And that's— good?

They wouldn't be encoded unless they had something to hide.

And you can crack it?

I think so.

SYSTEM ON

Cool.

RUNNIN PROGRA

Woah.

What?

Jaderoot? The Institution's using JADEROOT?

What? WHAT's JADEROOT?

It's a very rare, VERY poisonous plant, and it's pretty much only used in dark sorcery.

It's extremely corrosive and notoriously hard to control.

The Institution outlawed it a long time ago.

And yet these plans suggest that they've somehow got a large amount of it.

What are the plans FOR?

It seems they're trying to formulate a material that can store the jaderoot's poison without dissolving.

And judging by the size of these containers, that's a LOT of jaderoot.

If it's so rare, then where are they getting it all?

That's what I'm worried about.

If they're growing it themselves, they risk contaminating the entire kingdom's crops!

Crops? You're worried about the CROPS?

If it starts poisoning everyone's food, then yes.

Good point.

Not to mention whatever they're planning on DOING with all this jaderoot.

So you're not crazy, huh? The Institution really IS up to no good.

You thought I was crazy?

No, no, crazy in a GOOD way! Evil mad scientist kind of thing!

Just stop.

43

sip

Communications to Director.

INCOMING CALL

This had better be important, Rudy.

Turn on the news, Director. Channel six.

what's going on?

...these documents suggest that the Institution has been hoarding large quantities of a substance known as jaderoot...

SCANDAL!

SECRET DOCUMENTS LEAKED

...a rare and deadly poisonous plant commonly associated with dark magic, and which the Institution itself has banned.

46

ROYAL GUARD! DON'T MOVE!

where is the anchorwoman?

she went to Freshen up...

she could be anywhere. But she's not getting away this time.

THERE!

AFTER IT!

Haha oh man, you should've seen Goldenloin's face!

I stopped by the Institution on my way back.

They're flipping out!

These reports are entirely false.

It is a hoax, the work of the infamous Ballister Blackheart...

Think they'll convince anyone?

maybe. They're very good at covering things up.

It doesn't matter. That was only phase one.

YEAH! PHASES!

You did good, kid.

LATER...

This movie is absurd.

It makes no logical sense and the production values are appalling.

Gah!

Are you really scared of this?

You can take on a whole squadron of guards by yourself, and THIS is what scares you?

Well maybe if they'd been UNDEAD guards, it would have been a different story!

I don't understand what's so scary about zombies.

Reanimating the dead isn't hard, but they make TERRIBLE minions.

They can't move quickly and they fall to pieces in a matter of days.

Will you just watch the movie?!

AAAIIIII!

SPLORTCH

GLOMP

NYARGH

Oh come on! That is NOT what intestines look like!

SHUT UPPPPP

CHAPTER 6

ONE WEEK EARLIER

Whatcha making?

If you're going to come in here, GLOVES and GOGGLES.

grumble

CLATTER CRASH

Goggles. Gloves.

Now are you going to tell me what you're making?

It's the next phase of our plan.

Yes! Phases! Evil potions! This is what I'm talking about!

CAREFUL

so how are you going to get your super-fatal toxin out there?

Apples.

Apples?

Apples.

whoa, that's old-school villain right there. Are you pissed you're not the fairest of them all?

It's a classic.

We shouldn't need to plant too many — maybe a few dozen.

hum hum hum

That's all we'll need.

Once a few cases have broken out —

—people's imaginations will start to take over.

Apples planted, SIR!

Good. Now we wait.

For how long?

The toxin is time released. The effects won't become apparent for at least a few weeks.

Aw, boring.

We have to make absolutely sure no one traces it back to us.

In the meantime...

...how would you feel about robbing a bank?

POSITIVELY! I FEEL POSITIVELY ABOUT ROBBING A BANK!

I thought you might.

HIS MAJESTY'S ROYAL TREASURY

Hello, sir! Are you here to make a deposit?

Not quite.

We're here to make a withdrawal.

I can't open it. I'm not authorized.

You've done enough.

Better get out of here.

It's about to get messy.

All right, let's go.

Nimona!

WOOMP

see? I didn't Kill him!

Good job. Time to go.

what—

whoa.

FOOOOOM

OOF

CLINK

CLINK   CLINK

Blackheart.

Hello, Ambrosius.

You ready to split, Boss?

Come down and fight me, Villain!

Yeah, don't even think about it.

I KNOW, I wasn't GOING to—

FIGHT ME, YOU COWARD!

RAAAAAUUGH

what, are you
Robin Hood now?

No. I'm a
supervillain.

I Know you
are, Boss.

Aim for the wings.
Just bring them down.
I want them both
ALIVE.

KkcCHOOOM

I think NOT—

FFZ&ZZT

VRRRRRMMM

Haha oh man! That was awesome!

It went off without a hitch! And look at all this loot!

Ah— Nimona—

What?

Oh.

79

I thought I got them all — one must have slipped through!

BOSS, it's FINE.

NO, DON'T TOUCH IT!

You're such a GRANNY.

It's not even that deeAAAAAAAH!

I TOLD you not to touch it!

Ow ow ow ow ow ow ow

We have to get to my lab. I have medical supplies there.

It's bleeding a lot!

Will you stop SQUIRMING?

I'M SORRY, THAT MUST BE SO INCONVENIENT FOR YOU

This is all my fault. I never should have let this happen.

Boss, I said it's FINE.

It's not like I didn't know it would be dangerous.

Did you though? Did you REALLY?

I know this all seems like a big game to you, but the Institution doesn't play around.

They won't pull their punches just because you're young.

I'm not EXPECTING them to!

I appreciate your concern, but I've been looking out for myself for a long time.

So don't baby me, okay?

I just don't want you to get hurt!

Will you CHILL OUT?

No one ever got killed with one little arrow!

Actually, they do. That is kind of the PURPOSE of arrows.

And you need to stay off of that leg.

Aw, SERIOUSLY?

You're going to take it easy until it heals.

But what about all the evil plans!

It wouldn't hurt to lay low for a while.

UUUGGHH

So I'm stuck here with YOU until my leg gets better?

Afraid so.

Well, what's there to do around here, anyway?

Well, here we have World Domination; it builds strategy skills — you can play as a dog, a boot, or a trebuchet.

Bewilder builds language and observation skills...

I said I wanted to play VIDEO games.

Video games are a waste of time.

And board games AREN'T?

Why do you even have these? No one lives here but you!

I used to have some henchmen. Game night was a big hit.

Henchmen? What happened to them?

I can't work with mercenaries. It's impossible to build trust when they only care about their paychecks.

Oooh. Lemme guess. The Institution paid them off?

I don't want to talk about it.

World Domination, huh? I call the Scottie dog!

YES! a ten!

...eight...nine...ten!

Landing you in the Enchanted Forest, which is MY domain.

600 gold, please.

My Scottie dog will not pay your tyrannical toll!

Nimona...

He rallies the oppressed woodland creatures and organizes a revolt!

It just so happens I am a just ruler and greatly admired by all my subjects.

Squirrels scale the walls of the castle and bears batter down the gates!

Bloody chaos ensues!

The Enchanted Forest is ours!

Flick

I'm taking the 600 gold anyway.

HIGHWAY ROBBERY!

Plus another 600 for damages.

FOOOOOSh

That was fun! What do you want to do next?

84

HIS MAJESTY'S
HOSPITAL
MEDICAL ✠ CLINIC

I've never seen anything like this, Doctor.

Four cases in the last week alone!

They're not responding to any treatment we've tried.

We've run every test—but I don't know what to make of the results.

QUARANTINE

We don't know what's causing it. The patients have no ties to each other.

AUTHORIZED PERSONNEL ONLY

Do you remember that news report? The Institution's secret stash of Jaderoot, poisoning the Kingdom's crops?

But the Institution debunked that...

QUARANTINE

Yes... but suppose it's true?

I swear I will see them both captured and brought to justice...

Do I have to spell everything out for you?

RIOTS ERUPT

DISPOSE OF the sidekick.

What?

I'm not going to kill a little girl!

This is a matter of keeping your job. You think we can't replace you in an instant?

If this situation escalates any further, we will be forced to take drastic measures.

and your friend Blackheart WILL go down with her.

Blackheart is NOT my friend.

Right, archnemesis. of course.

And if you want him to REMAIN as such, you'll do as I say.

END OF CHAPTER SIX

CHAPTER 7

...Kingdom is in panic after the outbreak of a mysterious disease, rumored to be linked to experiments carried out by the Institution...

Meanwhile, Villain-at-large Ballister Blackheart's recent bank heist has caused mass withdrawals, forcing authorities to freeze all accounts...

LOOK WHAT I GOT YOU!

What's this?

I nicked it at the bank! Figured it would suit you!

C'mon, Boss, just picture it! When we've won, you'll be King, and I'll be your champion!

I never said I wanted to be King.

Who did you think was gonna take over after we ousted the Institution?

Or did you just not think that far ahead?

You're getting a little ahead of yourself. We're a long way from winning.

Yeah, but we WILL.

What makes you so sure?

Because you're a genius, DUH!

...you know I've never actually pulled one of these things off, right?

I don't exactly have the best track record.

Yeah, but THIS time, you have me!

You have to admit, we make a good team.

You have certainly proved your worth.

I think we should celebrate. I'm gonna make dinner!

You can cook? Or are you just looking for an excuse to blow up my kitchen?

Har har, I'm only the best cook EVER.

Nimona! Didn't I tell you to stay off that leg?

What do YOU want?

I need to talk to you.

Alone.

In person.

Can you meet me at the Antlered Snake tonight?

How stupid do you think I am?

It's not a trap, you have my word.

Your word is worth a lot, is it?

The Institution doesn't know about this, okay? I just want to talk.

We're talking now.

PLEASE, Ballister. It's important.

I'll buy the drinks.

...Fine.

Seven o'clock.

BOOP

Sigh

Nimona, I'm going out.

But what about dinner?

Just put mine in the fridge.

91

scoot

Remember when we used to come here every day after training?

I remember.

Well, I'm here. What do you want?

Where's your sidekick?

Is THAT what this is about?

Is she here?

she might be. You'd have no idea, would you?

I'D have no idea...

You've got to get rid of her.

Is that so? And, uh—

WHY WOULD I DO THAT.

The Institution is very displeased—

Yes, that was the idea.

Ballister—

The Institution is ordering me to KILL your sidekick.

94

I can't believe you're still hung up about that.

It was a long time ago, you know.

Besides, it was an ACCIDENT.

I bet you've said that so many times you've started to actually believe it.

It WAS!

It's just the two of us here, Ambrosius. You don't have to lie.

Wh—I'm not—everyone knows what happened that day! You're the only one who can't accept it!

Can't you just admit it, just this once?

You blew up my arm because you couldn't stand that I was better than you.

YOU WERE NEVER BETTER THAN ME!

BEEP

FSSSHH

Hey! You're home!

I put your dinner in the fridge like you said.

Whoa, what happened?

Did you get in a fight without me?

Tell me where they are! I'll mess their faces up!

BOSS?

I'm going to bed.

END OF
CHAPTER SEVEN

CHAPTER 8

SHUF

SCIENCE EXPO TODAY

BRILLIANT MINDS FROM ALL OVER THE LAND TO EXHIBIT AT KINGDOM'S ANNUAL FAIR

BEEP

What's this about?

Well, you seemed really depressed last night, so...

I thought some science would cheer you up!

You LOVE science!

We can't go to a big public event like this, Nimona. We're the two most wanted criminals in the kingdom.

I thought of that!

You're gonna need to put on this fake beard.

SCIENCE EXPO

ROBOT FIGHT

This beard itches.

Nimona, I really don't think this is going to fool anyone.

Well, it won't if you keep messing with it!

And my name's GREGOR.

Clearly I'm the only one taking this disguise thing seriously.

If we get caught it's YOUR fault.

Hey, this was your idea.

I haven't been here in years.

I used to dream about one day having my own booth here.

Ha, NERD.

So where should we...

Ooh! Churros!

Well hello there, young man!

One churro, please.

There you go!

But first— have you been good to your dad?

Yeah!

CHOMP CHOMP

He really takes after you, you know!

Oh—um— yes. I suppose he does.

CHURROS

DR. MORIBUND'S CREATURES

You have a good day now!

Carry me!

Hey!

Nimona, I'm not going to carry you.

Oh please, I carry you all the time!

And it's GREGOR.

Fine. But can you turn into something less ...heavy?

It's rude to comment on a lady's weight.

Is anyone looking?

No, you're fine.

Okay, that works.

Hello! I see that my Anomalous Energy Enhancer has caught your eye.

Well, I do like green glowing things.

I'm Dr. Meredith Blitzmeyer. Here's my card!

Ah. Yes. And I'm— Gregor.

So what does it do?

Well, right now, it... glows green.

That's it?

It's a new technology.

But this green glow does not come from electricity, nor flame, nor bioluminescence, nor any energy source hitherto known to man!

It needs no fuel, and its light will persist indefinitely!

Mm-hmm.

I understand your skepticism. I'm the only one researching anomalous energy, and this is all I have to show for it.

Anomalous energy?

It's based on a theory of my own invention!

I have made the journey over the mountains to the lands beyond, where the great sorcerers still practice their craft.

I observed their methods and noted that they seemed to draw their power from an invisible, apparently infinite source.

I theorized that there must be a vast field of energy that surrounds us all, but is only made detectable under very specific circumstances.

I dedicated myself to re-creating those circumstances scientifically!

This humble device, good sir, is the first step to reconciling science and magic!

Hm yes very interesting.

It will change the world! Infinite power, made available to everyone!

...oh.

FWEEEEEE

Well, it was nice talking to you, Doctor, but...

No, no, this shouldn't be happening...

BAM BAM

AHH!

FWSSSHHH

Well THAT'S never happened before...

HEY! YOU!

I've really got to go, Doctor!

Okay. Okay. They've definitely seen me. We need to get out of here.

huf
huf

You know what would be REALLY helpful?

IF YOU WERE ANYTHING OTHER THAN A CAT RIGHT NOW.

HISSSSSS

SWIPE

What are you saying, you're STUCK?

How can you be STUCK!

MRROW

What, and you can't talk? What's THAT about?

MMRRRAAGGHW

Ma! There's a crazy old hobo here talking to a cat!

I, uh — you see, I'm a scientist, and this is...

...a super-intelligent mutant cat.

What hobo! Where!

Get out of here, you crazy hobo!

I'm GOING!

Hold on. We're gonna make a break for it.

WOOP!

SLIP!

c'mere, you CAT!

AAHH

EEEEE

ZZZRRTT

Hey—
You okay?

Ngghhh.

WHAT THE
HECK WAS
THAT?!

SHHHH.
Can you get us
out of here?

Yeah, damn straight
I can. Hang on.

117

CRASH

Will you calm down?

NO.

That didn't go as well as it could have, but it's okay now.

You don't GET it!

I have NEVER lost my powers. I DON'T get STUCK.

It is NOT okay.

120

THUNK

Sorry about your kitchen.

Guess that'll come out of my paycheck too, huh?

END OF
CHAPTER EIGHT

CHAPTER 9

In today's news, six new patients were admitted to His Majesty's Hospital yesterday with reports of unpleasant and mysterious symptoms, bringing the total number of cases to twenty-three.

BREAKING NEWS

A link has been suggested between the illness and the Institution's supposed experimentation with the deadly substance jaderoot.

The king gave a press conference today on the subject of the epidemic, but failed to address these rumors.

Citizens are advised to avoid contact with infected parties, and examine all food for peculiar qualities before consuming it.

see that all infected parties are brought in for medical attention immediately.

And please remember to remain calm.

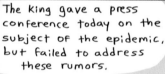

so that's good, huh?

Yes.

Everything's going according to plan?

I suppose it is.

you changed your hair?

Yeppp.

Hmmm.

what, you don't like it?

No, it's not that—it's just—

I thought pink was your color.

I like purple too.

Was there something you wanted?

No... I...

I wanted to make sure you were okay.

sure. why wouldn't I be?

Nimona.

I know something happened to you. Something you're not telling me.

You don't have to tell me if you don't want to.

I trust you, you know. And you can trust me.

You know that, right?

BOSS.

It's fine, okay? Just let it go.

...okay.

Are you hungry? I thought maybe we could order a pizza.

Sure.

Any particular toppings you want?

Nah, you pick.

Sardines it is, then.

Don't you DARE put sardines on that pizza.

Blackheart is past the point of being controlled. I want him out of the picture.

I'm telling you, he can still be useful to us!

That isn't your call.

You're already asking me to kill a young girl. If the public finds out you're sending me out on assassinations...

The public's opinion is not a priority right now.

If Blackheart dies, he'll be a hero for the commoners!

Arrest him, pin the poisonings on him...

Really, Goldenloin, do you fancy yourself sly?

Your motivations are quite transparent. I KNOW what the nature of your relationship was.

I made it clear at the time that I disapproved.

If your fixation on him has impeded your ability to do your job, then he truly has outlived his usefulness.

We'll find you a new nemesis.

Perhaps you will be more competent without Blackheart as a distraction.

I won't kill him.

If you demand I kill the girl, I'll do it — but I won't kill him.

Very well.

Guarantee the termination of the sidekick, take Blackheart into custody, and he will live.

Do we have an accord?

Yes, Director.

Good. Come this way. I have something for you.

You're clearly outmatched the way things are now, so let's even the field.

Shock-absorbent plating, robotically enhanced performance, electrical stun units in the gauntlets. It should be quite sufficient to subdue a half-mechanical man and a little girl.

You'll select a team to go with you. They'll be similarly outfitted.

I don't want any mistakes this time.

Should I lead an attack on his fortress?

It would be unwise to stage the conflict on his own turf.

We need to draw him out. Engage him on our own terms.

A trap? Ballister won't fall for that. He's too paranoid.

Hmm, perhaps.

It would not surprise me if he had become a little...overly confident these days, however.

ROYAL
TOURNAMENT
COME ONE · COME ALL
-Jousting-
-melee-
-archery-

FEATURING
the
Kingdom's champion
SIR AMBROSIUS
GOLDENLOIN

TOU
COME

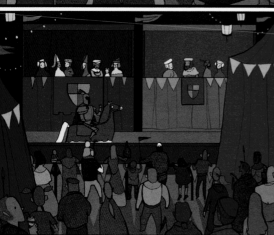

Do they really think that this will appease people?

I don't know, I think we could all use a little fun.

This is just asking for trouble, if you ask me.

Boss, we have a problem.

129

Found it!

Enjoy!

On one side, Knight errant Sir Coriander Cadaverish!

And on the other, representing the Institution— Sir Mansley Girthrod!

BOOOO o

BOOOOOO

BOOOO

"Any sign of Blackheart yet?"

"None yet, Director."

"He'll show, I'm sure of it."

"What's going on over there?"

"Ma'am?"

"Unbelievable."

133

People of the Kingdom.

My name is Ballister Blackheart, but I'm sure you know that already.

You may think of me as your enemy, but I have only ever fought against the Institution, not against you.

Your true enemies are the ones who have beaten you down and kept you in compliance through fear.

They took your children and raised them as soldiers. They mongered war at the expense of their people.

They've locked us into a system where they hold all the power.

In return, they promised you safety, but they've broken that promise.

In their quest for war, they've endangered the very people they swore to protect.

They took away your power.

It's time to take it back.

138

I've traced the signal of Blackheart's transmission.

It's coming from the communications terminal back at headquarters.

Attempting to access security cameras.

Security cameras have been disabled. Guards on duty not responding.

He's definitely there.

Do you hear that, Goldenloin?

Copy that, Director.

Get in there and TAKE HIM DOWN.

As to the rest of you, get this crowd under control.

By any means necessary.

142

143

WARNING. FULL LOCKDOWN IN PROGRESS.

CLANK

CLANK

CLANK

CLANG

Ha! It's another trap! A DOUBLE trap!

Those walls are reinforced steel. Not even YOU could break through them!

Yeah, you wanna bet?

Step aside, Blackheart.

It's the sidekick we want. Give her up and you needn't be harmed.

A double trap. Clever. I'll give you that one.

However, it seems to me — you're stuck in this trap right along with us.

Ah, but we came prepared.

Bring it on.

RAAUUGH

BAM BAM BAM

ZKKT

NIMONA!

KICK

I got 'er —

GUH

RAUGHHH

NIMONA!

ZZZKT

Goldenloin to Director. It's done.

LOCKDOWN COMPLETE. PLEASE STAND BY.

CLANK

CLANK

sorry, Ballister.

156

157

BAM

Will you stop...breaking... all my doors...

Let go. I can stand.

Geez, fine. There you go. Knock yourself out.

Whoa!

I didn't mean ACTUALLY knock yourself out.

Augh— my HEAD—

What happened— I don't — How did we—

Don't worry about it.

No—no—they KILLED you. You were DEAD.

Obviously not.

I SAW. I SAW it happen.

Relax. It was a trick. To get them to lift the lockdown.

A trick— but how—

I said don't worry about it.

Goldenloin— is he— did you—

What was I supposed to do? He was trying to kill US.

Nimona, IS HE DEAD?

I don't know.

I'll go find out!

You can't go back out there! It's too dangerous!

NIMONA!

161

We did everything we could, Director. We didn't have a chance.

She's far more powerful than we thought.

She can't be KILLED.

We assumed she was a girl disguised as a monster, but she's not.

She's a monster disguised as a girl.

I am not interested in excuses. I saw the footage.

You didn't see what I saw.

You didn't see her FACE.

I don't even think Ballister's the one calling the shots anymore. I think she's controlling him somehow.

Whatever the case may be, it is no longer your concern.

You're being replaced.

What are you going to do? You can't FIGHT her.

Fighting her is no longer the plan.

VOIP

END OF CHAPTER NINE

CHAPTER 10

Boss?

Oh, there you are.

Where have YOU been?!

Geez, will you chill out? I TOLD you I was going out to scout around.

What is your problem lately? You've been acting seriously weird all week.

It's looking pretty bleak out there.

You were right, they're definitely censoring the news channels.

They've got the rioters from the tournament locked up—couldn't find out where. Nobody knows.

And here's the kicker—

Two of the people infected with your virus have died.

WHAT?

Whoa!

That's IMPOSSIBLE. I engineered it to be nonlethal!

Well, maybe it's some OTHER mysterious illness then.

But the point is, they're dead.

This has gone on long enough. We have to get the cure to them.

Are you KIDDING?

This is great for us!

Panic is at an all-time high!

Everyone hates the Institution right now!

There won't be a better time to strike. They're disorganized, their star player is in disgrace...

We should attack now and take power from them once and for all.

THEN you can cure the sick people. They'll think you're awesome!

No.

No one else is going to die.

I'm no more fit to rule than the Institution is.

I'm a liar and murderer, and I'm done with this.

169

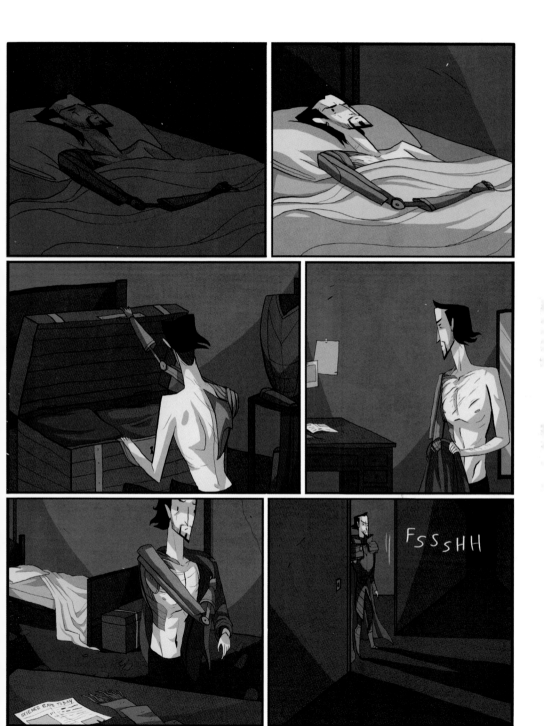

FSSSHH

whrrrrr
whrrrr

whrrrrr
whrrrr

CONTACTS

SIR GOLDENLOIN

INSTITUTION - DIRECT

NIMONA

CALL FAILED

NIMONA

UNABLE
TO
CONNECT

whrr rr
whrrrr

MEREDITH
BLITZMEYER

MAGICAL
SCIENTIST*

101 - 0112 - r070

*NOT A WITCH

CALLING

BLITZMEYER
LABS

Yes? Hello! who is it?

Hello, Doctor. We met at the science fair— you gave me your card.

Oh! Gregor, was it? You've cut your beard!

Actually, my name is Ballister Blackheart.

Is it? That's nice.

You don't... recognize me?

I've been on the news a lot lately.

Ah, I don't watch the news! A waste of time.

Is there something I can help you with?

Yes. I just wanted to know...

You said you've journeyed to the lands beyond the mountains. To the places where magic still thrives.

You must have come across many strange creatures in your travels.

Have you encountered many — shapeshifters?

Oh yes, some.

What kind? Werewolf? Selkie?

Not exactly...

A being who can take on the form of any living creature in a matter of seconds.

Who can be a dragon one moment and a cat the next.

That can even grow back limbs if they're cut off—even its head.

You know, hypothetically speaking.

Well, I imagine that such a beast would be impossible to detect or track.

It's very rare that the powers of skin-walkers and those of doppelgängers overlap at all — and that's without even touching on on the regeneration.

Although— hm.

That DOES sound something like the beast Gloreth slew, doesn't it?

You do know the legend of Gloreth, yes?

Of course. I am — I was a Knight.

She slew a dragon though, didn't she?

That's a mistranslation. The original text refers to only a "scaled beast" or a "great serpent."

Accounts from local villagers refer to its ability to change its shape and size, and claimed that it would walk among them in various human and animal forms.

They say it couldn't be harmed with sword or arrow.

There's even a theory among certain circles that the beast KILLED Gloreth that day and took her place.

And by "certain circles" you mean... message board conspiracy theorists?

Well, yes naturally.

175

176

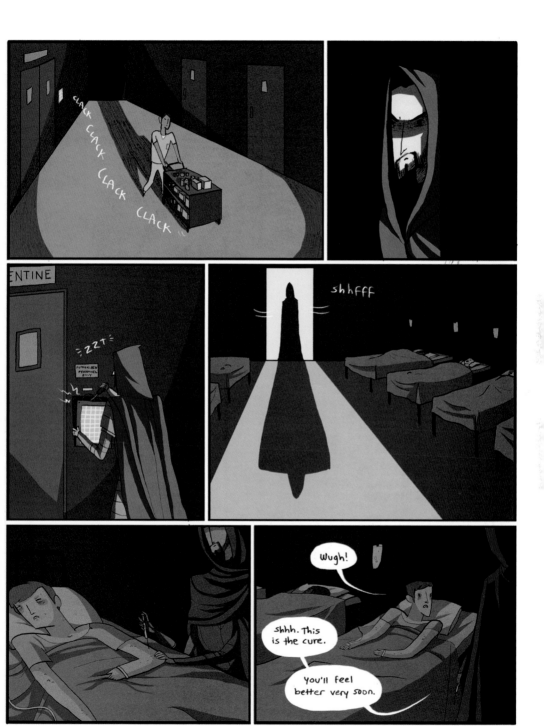

There you go.

BALLISTER BLACKHEART!

YOU ARE SURROUNDED.

COME OUT WITH YOUR HANDS UP.

QUARANTINE

ZZZKT

vugghh...

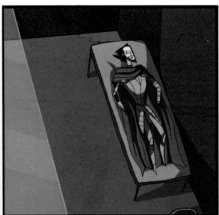

You awake?

You.

They really couldn't find anyone else to guard me?

Why are you on guard duty, anyway? Seems below your rank...

sore spot?

Where's your sidekick, Ballister?

This again.

She's gone. Are you happy?

Gone where?

I don't know. She LEFT. She's not coming back.

Well, THAT's a relief.

It looks like you got what you wanted after all.

I'm glad she's gone. You're better off.

She was vicious, she was cruel, she was— EVIL.

So am I.

We both know that's not true.

How'd we end up like this?

You blew up my arm, for one.

...you really do have to bring that up every time, don't you?

Yes.

I just meant... there was a time. Before.

Things were simpler. We were together. It was... good.

And YOU always remember them as WORSE.

Oh, DO I?

you BETRAYED me. You SHOT me.

It was never that good.

you always remember things as better than they were.

I—I never wanted to hurt you, I—

I didn't— It was—

Don't you dare try to tell me again that it was an accident.

It wasn't.

The night before the joust— the Director called me to her office.

She told me that I had promise. That I was her choice for the Institution's champion.

But she said I'd have to prove myself against you in the joust, or that chance would go away.

I wanted it, more than anything. You never wanted it as much as me.

You were just BETTER, without hardly even seeming to try.

Then... on the day of the joust...

This isn't my lance.

Director says it is your lance.

No, it's NOT.

It's weaponized— what does she expect me to do with a weaponized lance?

She expects you to win.

I had no intention of actually USING it...

I was a good rider — you remember.

I knew I could win.

But the new lance was too heavy — it threw me off-balance.

I don't even remember — but I must have —

I'm sorry, Ballister. I'm so sorry.

183

Ballister...

WOOP WOOP WOOP WOOP

RED ALERT. REQUESTING ADDITIONAL PERSONNEL TO SECTION B3. REQUIRED SECURITY CLEARANCE LEVEL SEVEN.

WOOP WOOP WOOP WOOP WOOP WOOP WOOP

What's going on?

Goldenloin to Communications. What's the cause of the alarm? Do you need me to report?

Negative. The situation is under control. Stay where you are.

But what's—

≈CLK≈

No one tells me anything.

185

This armor is atrocious. I hate it.

Do you remember how they used to make us wear that old training armor and they never cleaned it?

This smells like that.

I don't want to talk to you, Ambrosius.

I remember it smelled so bad it made you throw up in the helm.

I didn't do that.

Yes you did!

No, that was— what's his name— Garamond.

Garamond! I forgot about him. He was awful.

Why did you think that was me?

I could've sworn it was you who did that.

I wish— we could just go back. I wish things could be how they were.

We can't. It will never be the same again.

You chose to play along all these years. That doesn't just go away.

Come on. Director's sent for Blackheart.

Where are we?

I don't know. I've never been here before.

Will you stop fraternizing with the enemy?!

Care to show me some respect?

Why should I? I outrank you now.

Clearance code zero-four-nine-six. We have Blackheart.

Will you two pipe down? Now is not the time.

BEEP

Come on, let's go.

WHAM WHAM WHAM WHAM WHAM WHAM WHAM

What's that noise...?

What is this place?

shut up.

Welcome, Lord Blackheart.

Why did you bring me here? What is all this?

I thought you'd be impressed. We've built up quite a collection over the years.

We're on the cutting edge of weapons development.

Weapons! For what purpose? The kingdom is not at war.

Surely a tactical mind such as your own can appreciate the value of a deterrent.

A dangerous nation is a powerful nation.

Are you CRAZY, Director, or just stupid?

It's not going to hold her forever.

What do you think will happen when she gets out?

She's not going to get out.

ZZKKT

AAAAHHH!

BOSS!

groan...

There. You see?

You can take our shocks indefinitely, can't you? But I doubt he can.

A few more of those and he'll be dead. So I suggest you behave.

Nimona... it's okay...

I'm glad you've decided to be reasonable.

ZZRRT

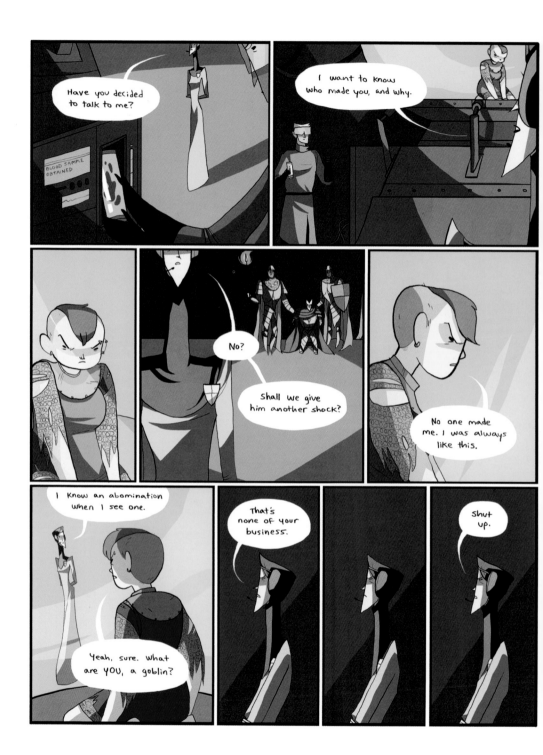

shock him again.

NO!

ZKKKTT

Don't you touch him again!

Guards, please remove Goldenloin from this room. I will deal with him later.

TRAITOR—

Get your hands OFF me!

Nnnn...

Heh.

How's that blood sample looking so far?

Can't see anything special about it myself.

Computer, what's your read on this?

SCANNING SAMPLE.

SCAN RESULT: BLOOD SAMPLE, HUMAN, TYPE AB POSITIVE.

Weird.

There should be some kind of irreg- aaAAAAI

What is it?!

I — it — EXPLODED...

It's — it's growing.

WARNING, EXTREME ACTIVITY DETECTED. OVERLOAD IMMINENT.

— she's still got control over the cells.

AAAHHH!!

Ballister!

RAAAAAAUGHH

Nim—

come ON!

FOOOOSHH

What do you think you're doing?

You can't FIGHT her, Ambrosius, not like that. We've ESTABLISHED this.

What am I supposed to do? She's going to kill a lot of people if we don't stop her.

We have to get back down to the lab—Nimona is still in there!

No, Nimona is out THERE, about to destroy the Kingdom!

Part of her is— but part of her never left the cage.

If I can get her out—I can talk to her. Calm her down.

She almost KILLED you, Ballister. She was about to burn you to a crisp.

What makes you think she'll listen to you now?

She's never been exactly STABLE. And now she's really angry.

Oh, and what reason would she have for being ANGRY, I wonder?!

207

She's not herself. The dragon — it grew from a few cells. It's a mindless beast born of pure rage.

But the rest of her is still there. I saw her. That's the part I can talk to.

She's alone down there... she'll think I abandoned her...

Really? After everything we saw in there, you still think she's just a scared little girl?

We're wasting time. It's already started.

Innocent people are DYING, Ballister. THEY need our help, not some IMMORTAL MONSTER.

Ambrosius, she WILL kill you. There is NO scenario where you win.

I never did anything good my whole life. Maybe I can't defeat her but I have to TRY.

Stop... wait.

There... there may be a device that can shut down her powers for a while.

208

You can't prioritize her life over theirs.

She's a killer, Ballister. She's always been a killer.

Whether or not you decide to help me, I've got to do SOMETHING.

...No. I can still save her.

I can save them all.

I need to find the device first. Do NOT confront her until I do. She WILL kill you.

You want to be a hero, concentrate on getting the people in the city to safety.

Do you still have that fancy armor?

Somewhere, yes.

You might want to go get it.

END OF
CHAPTER TEN

CHAPTER 11

PAT
PAT

How can
I help?

Your Anomalous
Energy Enhancer.

I need to
borrow it.

You need to borrow
my life's work.

Yes.

My only
prototype.

It's very
important.

I have reason to
believe it may hamper
her abilities.

It may be the
only thing that can
stop her.

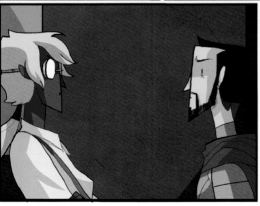

Okay,
but you BETTER
not break it.

Come on, then! Have at it!

RAAAUGH

CHOOOM

Let's see you grow back from THIS!

FZZKKT

FFFOOOM

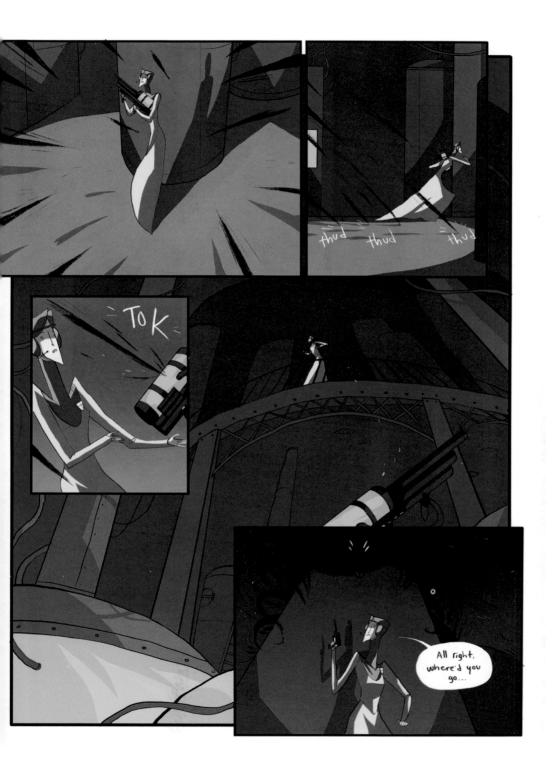

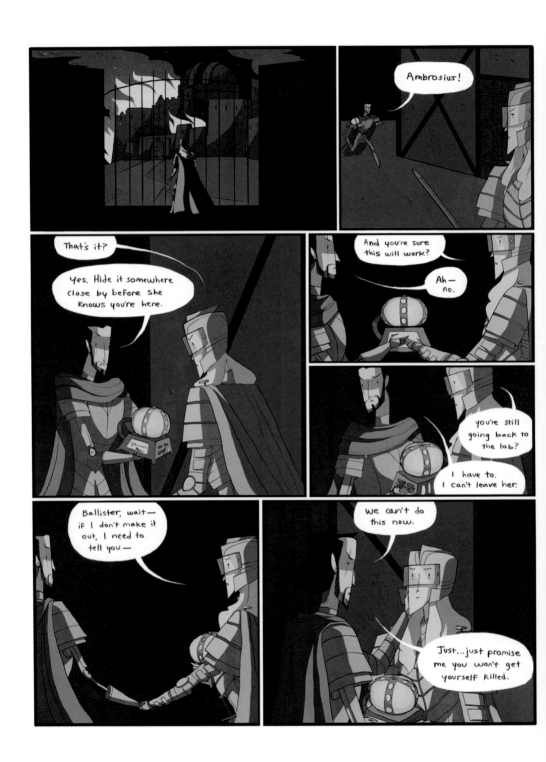

Half the village saw it happen.

Some even say they saw her breathe fire.

The villagers think she's possessed.

Her parents have a different theory.

They claim that at birth, their daughter was feeble and sick, not expected to live long.

Until, after one particularly dire illness, she quickly recovered and grew into a healthy, robust girl.

Her parents thought nothing of it at the time.

But now they claim this child is an imposter.

That their natural child—the sickly one—is dead, and in its place—something else.

We're going to need a stronger enclosure than this.

Is that really necessary? I mean...

...she's just a kid.

Where's my mom and dad? I want to go home.

Your parents brought you here, didn't they? Why do you think they did that?

I—I burnt a man...

I killed them. The raiders.

But they wanted to kill us FIRST. I saved everybody.

And how did you do that?

I don't know.

You're not going home. Not until you're better. Do you want to get better?

Yes. Then can I see my mom and dad?

Of course.

We'll have her moved to our facility in the morning. Don't upset or excite her in the meantime.

We'll take care of the rest.

225

NIMONA!

nnnNNOOO!

Go away! Just leave me ALONE!

Nimona, it's me, it's just me. You KNOW me.

...don't you?

...Boss?

You...you came back.

OF course I did.

come on, let's get you out of here.

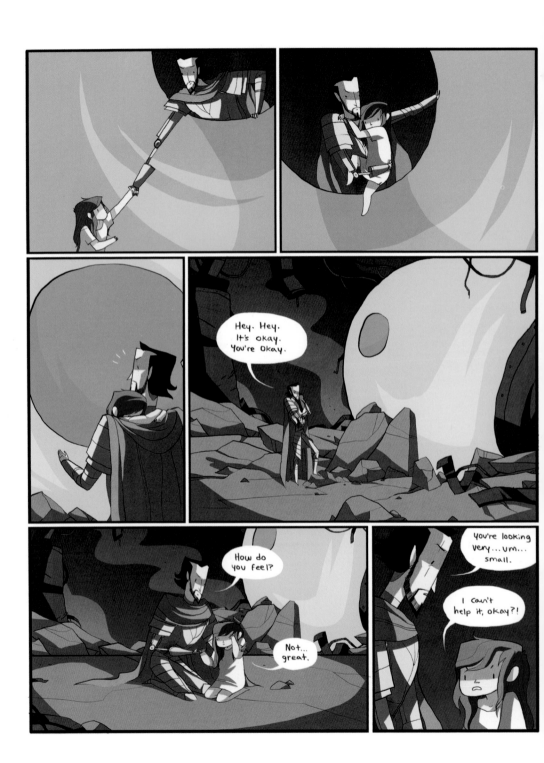

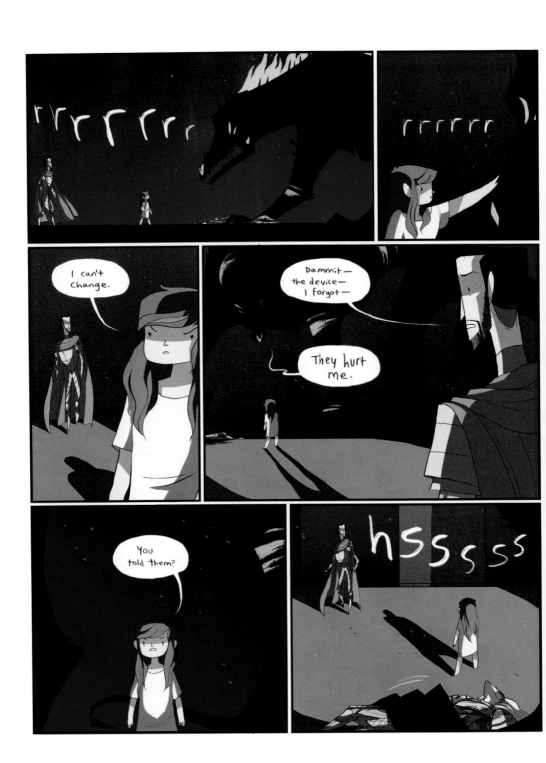

238

242

Nimona!

WARNING. JADEROOT MELTDOWN IMMINENT. ACTIVATING PURGE PROTOCOL.

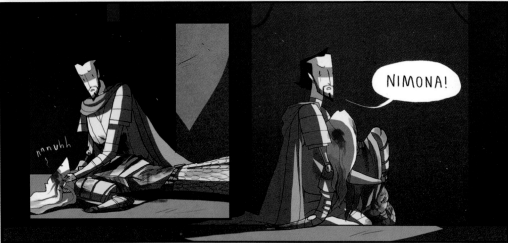

mmuhh

NIMONA!

PURGE WILL OCCUR IN TEN MINUTES.

EVACUATE PREMISES AND MAINTAIN 500-FOOT DISTANCE.

He needs a hospital immediately.

Auughh...

Lord Blackheart, what happened? Is the beast slain? Is it over?

Yes.

The Kingdom is in shock after the murderous rampage of a mysterious beast last night that resulted in the deaths of the King and the Director of the Institution.

They are only two out of an extensive list of casualties.

Sir Ambrosius Goldenloin and former villain turned champion of the people Ballister Blackheart brought down the beast early this morning, ending a night of terror.

Both are in the hospital after injuries sustained during the attack. Sir Goldenloin remains in critical condition.

The beast's origins remain unknown, although testimony from surviving employees at Institution headquarters suggests it may be an escaped Institution experiment gone awry.

The catastrophe has brought to light many of the Institution's illegal projects, including the stockpiling of massive quantities of jaderoot.

Prominent voices are already clamoring for the permanent disbanding of the Institution.

Despite this tragedy, we remain united.

We will stay strong, and we will rebuild.

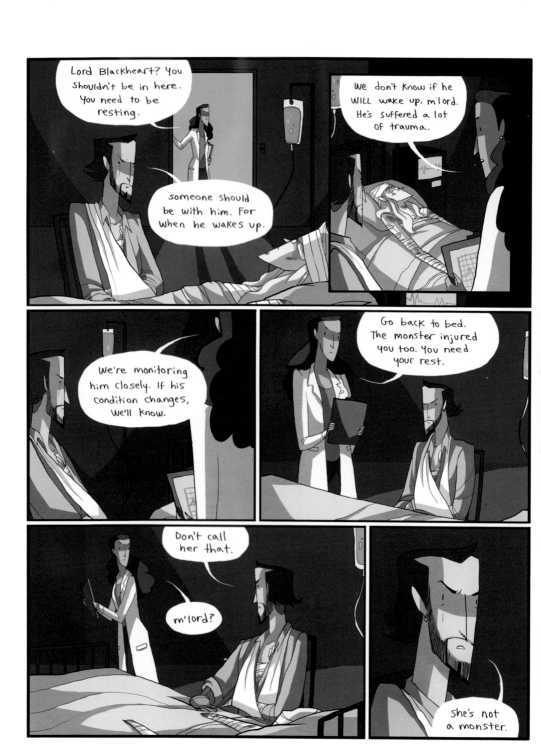

Gregor?

Doctor!

Did you really put me as your emergency contact?

I don't have a lot of friends, okay?

Doctor, your device— it was destroyed. I'm sorry.

Never mind. I'll build another one.

I hear you're some sort of hero!

Not me, no.

You did what you had to do, then?

You saved a lot of people.

But I couldn't save her.

EPILOGUE

Of course... I still wonder...

About every cat who watch me too closely

...about every stranger who gives me a knowing look.

I can only hope I reached her in some small way.

I can only hope that if she does come back...

She'll know me for who I am.

A friend.

THANK

YOU!!!

Thanks to my parents and my family for always supporting me and for pushing me to do the things they knew I could do. To Aimee, for always being there to talk me through narrative binds and to give me a shoulder to cry on when I needed one. To Taylor, for always being willing through the years to listen to whatever story I was on fire with at the time. To Charlie and Andrew, for showing incredible faith in a first-time comic creator to bring this book to life. To my sister, for motivating me to tell a better story. To Stephen, for helping me create an online home for Nimona and calmly fielding more than his fair share of panicked emails. To Joan, under whose patient instruction I created the first ten pages and who encouraged me to take the story through to the end. To Esme, Alfred, Sprouts, 2ft1st, redsky, soniadelvalle, Nexus427, Daniel Stubbs, Erin, Joel, FevversAB, Samantha, Rob, Eric, Bear, stickfigurefairytales, Arianod, Spoilersss, Laur, Idris.Ababa, Chris Bishop, ТЯЦТНӨЯDΛЯϹ, and all the rest of the Tinfoil Brigade, for filling the comments section with lively and good-natured dialogue every week and whose enthusiasm gave me strength. To everyone who supported this comic through the years in such a variety of ways, without whom this story would almost certainly not exist the way it does now. Thank you all, and I love you very much.

The following mini-comics originally appeared in the web comic as Christmas Specials in December 2012 and December 2013.

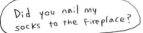

I GOT YOU A PRESENT

A scarf!

I made it!

I turned into a sheep and knitted it from my own wool.

wait, what?

knitting with hooves is hard but I got the hang of it.

MERRY CHRISTMAS!
From Nimona & Ballister

259

CHRISTMAS
at the INSTITUTION

CHRISTMAS SPECIAL 2013

BALLISTERRR

what is it?

THOSE BIG DOLTS TOOK MY STOCKING!

your what?

MY STOCKING. MY CHRISTMAS STOCKING.

How is Father Christmas going to bring me presents without a stocking?!

okay, calm down. we'll get it back.

I'll call my dad. He'll have them ARRESTED.

you don't have a dad.

Do too. He's rich and lives in a castle far away.

Everyone knows you made that up.

This is why people hit you.

HEY! GIVE HIM BACK HIS STOCKING!

stocking? you mean my fashionable SOCK?

GASP!

YOU VILLAIN!

What are you gonna do, AMB-RO-ZEE-US?

That's not even an insulting nickname, that's — just his name.

I couldn't think anything up 'cause it's stupid enough as it is.

I'LL HAVE YOUR HEAD!

Whatever, have your stupid sock.

Everyone knows Father Christmas doesn't bring gifts to orphans like us.

Maybe it's just because you've been NAUGHTY!

C'mon, Ambrosius.

Look, you shouldn't get your hopes up too much, in case he doesn't come...

He will!

I mean...he hasn't yet...but maybe this year he will.

Stay and wait for Father Christmas with me!

I have to go back to my room, Ambrosius. Anyway, the sooner you fall asleep, the sooner he'll come.

ZZZZZ

THE END

DEVELOPMENT OF NIMONA

woop

Sir Ambrosius Goldenloin   Lord Ballister Blackheart

I'm your new SIDEKICK

NO.

I don't wanna be kept don't wanna be caged
don't wanna be damned oh hell

I don't wanna be broke don't wanna be saved
don't wanna be S.O.L.

hissssss